ARE YOU A BABY REINDEER?

Written by Jennifer V. Chatman

Illustrated by Kristina Djenadic

Jennifer V. Chatman
2018

This book is dedicated to my husband Chris who works hard every day to teach me to be a bigger dreamer. To my sons Liam and Colin, and daughter Caroline, who give me a reason to want to be brave enough to try new adventures and to see the possibility of failing only as the potential to learn. The four of them own my heart in every possible way.

Farmer Jack was out walking the edge of his farm, checking that things were just as they should be. He heard a rustling ten paces ahead, so he went to see what was making the noise. There, against a small stack of wood, nestled in a pile of leaves, was a little family.

Winter was coming on fast as it was just days before Thanksgiving. In these parts, snow would be on its way. You could almost smell it in the air.

Farmer Jack loaded the little family into the back of his truck to take them to the local shelter. "These little ones might just brighten someone's Christmas," he thought. So Farmer Jack and his sweet cargo headed down the road.

The little family bounced around in the back of the truck. The country road was full of rocks and sticks that made the truck jump up and down with noisy bangs and clanks. One nosy little fellow got a little too curious and stood against the back to get a better look at what was going on. With one huge BUMP, the little guy lost his balance and was dumped out of the truck.

He hit the ground with a massive thud that sent surprise through his tiny body. When he finally stood to shake the cobwebs from his head, he realized that the truck was out of reach. He watched the truck drive out of view; no truck, no farmer and no family.

"Oh, what to do?" he thought. He decided to follow the road. Surely he would catch up.

The little one started out. One foot in front of the other, one foot in front of the other. He walked and walked until he needed a rest. He sat still trying to hear the truck that held his family. But instead he heard a small voice ask,

"Are you a baby reindeer?"

The little guy looked up to find a small squirrel gnawing on an acorn. "Well, I'm not quite sure what I am. How would I know if I was a baby reindeer?" he asked.

Tossing the acorn aside, the squirrel said, "Oh, reindeer are very brave animals. They can fly through the air bringing toys to children all over the world at Christmas time. I just thought, you are very brave to be so small and be on the road all by yourself. You must be a baby reindeer."

The little one said, "I really don't know about being brave, I just need to keep moving to find my family." With that he continued on his way down the road.

The day was growing old, so the little one decided to stop for a sleep. "Surely I'll find my family in the morning," he thought. "Let me just rest for a bit." And the little guy curled up for the night.

Morning arrived and it was time to stand and stretch his legs when the little guy felt a tiny body next to his and heard a tinier little yawn.

Are you a baby reindeer?" the tiny voice said.

"Well, I'm not quite sure what I am. How would I know if I was a baby reindeer?" he asked.

His new friend was the smallest of field mice. The mouse snuggled closer to his friend and said, "Oh, reindeer are very warm creatures. They can endure the coldest weather with their great warm bodies, so that they can help deliver toys to children all over the world at Christmas time. I just thought," as he snuggled even closer, "You are so warm and soft, you must be a baby reindeer."

The little one said, "I really don't know about being warm, I just need to keep moving to find my family." And with a long warm hug, the mouse said goodbye to his very warm friend, who continued to walk down the rocky road.

By this time in his journey, the little one was growing quite hungry. He spied a single shiny, red apple lying on the road. He crunched his first bite when he heard something rustle in the leaves. It was a small rabbit whose fur looked to be changing from brown to white. The rabbit said, "Oh. Do you see any other apples lying around? I'm so very hungry and the rest of the apples still cling to the tree."

 Looking around, the little guy said, "I do not see any more apples on the ground, but please, please share the one that I have." The rabbit hopped over, beaming with gratitude, and took his half of the apple. Chomping away, the rabbit asked, **"Are you a baby reindeer?"**

"Well, I'm not quite sure what I am. How would I know if I was a baby reindeer?" he asked.

Holding the apple close to his heart, the rabbit said, "Oh, reindeer are very kind animals. They give of themselves to help deliver toys to children all over the world at Christmas time. I just thought," as he looked sweetly at his apple half, "you were so kind to share the only apple, you must be a baby reindeer."

The little guy said, "I really don't know about being kind, I just need to keep moving to find my family." He finished his apple, quickly cleaned his paws and face, waved goodbye to his new friend and headed on his way.

The road began to curve into a short stretch of shade. The little one decided to stop and stretch for a bit. It had been a long day of walking and he needed to take a break. He did some loooonnnnggg stretches, and shakes and wiggles. He caught sight of his tail and began spinning and spinning in circles to try to catch it. He stopped when he heard giggling coming from the tree above.

The voice from above stop laughing long enough
to ask, **"Are you a baby reindeer?"**

"Well, I'm not quite sure what I am. How would I know if
I was a baby reindeer?" he asked.

Swooping down from the tree to land on a giant stump,
a great owl spread his wings and said, "Oh, reindeer
are animals that bring happiness to others. They bring
joy to many by helping to deliver toys to children all
over the world at Christmas time. I just thought..."
He stopped to double over in laughter again. "I just
thought how happy I was watching you twirl in circles,
you must be a baby reindeer."

The little one said, "I really don't know about bringing
happiness, I just need to keep moving to find my
family." He smiled and bowed farewell to the owl and
continued on his way through the short shady stretch.

Just beyond the trees, the road opened to a clearing. There was a house nestled just off the road with a young boy sitting on the front steps. The boy looked so sad. He sat still, staring at his sneakers.

The little boy was new to these parts. His family had moved from the city and was setting up house in the country. They had only been there for a few weeks and the boy was having a hard time in this strange new place.

The little one was growing weary by this time. He had walked and walked but was now feeling sad that he might never find his family. He wandered up to the steps where the boy was sitting, as that looked like as good a place as any to rest.

The boy was so surprised by this new arrival. The little one climbed up one step, then two, and sat right down close to the boy and stared at the boy's sneakers too. The boy could feel the warmth of the little body next to him. He slowly lifted his hand so that his new friend could give him a sniff. After a bit the boy began petting the soft fur of his new companion and was rewarded with a lick under the bottom of his chin.

The next thing you know, the two were running and wrestling together in the yard, both having the time of their lives. Seeing the two new friends from the window, the boy's mother rushed out of the house to witness the new friendship. The little one ran to her and sat at attention at her feet.

"Well who is this?" she exclaimed. "What a **brave** little one you are, out here all alone. How **warm** and soft you are!" she said as she petted his mottled brown fur. "It is so **kind** of you to visit us on this cold, cold day. You deserve a warm blanket and a treat for **bringing happiness** to my little boy, for I haven't heard him laugh in weeks."

And as the three walked toward the house,
the little one thought, "Brave, Warm, Kind,
brings Happiness.....GASP!"

"I AM A BABY REINDEER!"

Made in the USA
Columbia, SC
07 December 2018